Abe and Zeek

by Liza Charlesworth

ISBN: 978-1-338-84449-8

Art Director: Tannaz Fassihi; Designer: Cynthia Ng; Illustrated by Michael Robertson
Copyright © Liza Charlesworth. All rights reserved. Published by Scholastic Inc.

2 3 4 5   68   26 25 24

Printed in Jiaxing, China. First printing, June 2022.

His name is Abe!

His name is Zeek!

Abe made a rule:
"Abe has an A. Zeek has a Z.
So I go first all the time."

3

Race, race!
They ran to a red bike.
Abe got on it first.

4

Race, race!
They ran to a nice boat.
Abe got on it first.

5

Race, race!
They ran to a cute mule.
Abe got on it first.

Race, race!
They ran to a fake toad.
Abe got on it first.

Abe made his pal Zeek mad.
Mad, mad, mad!
Mad, mad, mad!

Abe made his pal Zeek yell,
"I DO NOT LIKE YOUR RULE!
IT IS NOT NICE!"

9

"OK," said Abe.
"You can go first in a line
to get ice cream."

10

Wait! Abe did NOT
make his pal Zeek mad.
Zeek got a lime cone.
Abe got a peach cone.

11

Race, race!
They ran to a neat jeep.
"We can both go
on it first!" said Abe.

So Abe and his pal Zeek
rode in the neat jeep
side by side.
BEEP, BEEP!

Read & Review

Invite your learner to point to each long-vowel word and read it aloud.

a_e

Abe name
made race
fake make

i_e

like bike
time ice lime
line
nice side

o_e

cone
rode

14

u_e

cute
rule
mule

ee

Zeek jeep
beep

ai

wait

ea

neat cream
peach

oa

boat
toad

15

Fun Fill-Ins

Read the sentences aloud, inviting your learner to complete them using the long-vowel words in the box.

> rule   side   Zeek   boat   Abe

1. This story is about Abe and _____.

2. "I go first all the time!" said _____.

3. Zeek did not like Abe's _____.

4. Abe went first on a bike and _____.

5. At the end, Abe AND Zeek ride in a jeep side by _____.